Adventures in His Story

Book

BACK T BEGINNING

Written by Jen Decker

Illustrated by Nifty Illustration

To all the kiddos who will read this book.

Written by Jennifer Decker

www.adventuresinhisstory.com

adventuresinhisstory@gmail.com

Illustrated by Nifty Illustration

www.niftyillustration.com

niftyillustration@mail.com

ISBN 979-8-9858333-0-0 (paperback)

ISBN 979-8-9858333-1-7 (hardcover)

Table of Contents

1

IN THE BEGINNING

"Hurry Tommy!" said Janie. "Mom says we have to open our gifts from Pastor Jack at the *same* time."

"Whatever," said Tommy. He ran his hands over and around the gift. "It just feels like a dumb book Janie."

"C'mon Tommy!" cried Janie. "I want to see what it is."

She's not going to stop, thought Tommy. It's no fun being a twin, especially with a nine-year-old girl. He followed Janie into her room.

They sat together on the floor and tore off the wrapping paper.

"See, they're just books Janie," said Tommy. "They're not even different. We both got the exact same book."

"They're Bibles Tommy!" cried Janie with glee. "Now I have my very own Bible and I won't have to borrow Moms."

Yip dee dip, thought Tommy.

Janie ran her hand over the cover of her new Bible. The pink leather felt smooth.

"They're not the exact same book Tommy," said Janie. "Mine is pink and yours is brown."

Tommy rolled his eyes. Janie excitedly opened to the first page and began to read aloud to her brother:

*In the beginning God created the
heavens and the earth.*

A little bit down the page she read:

*God said, let there be light; and there
was light.*

And then she read:

*God said, let the water be gathered into
one place and let dry land appear.*

"Isn't that amazing Tommy?" asked
Janie.

"It sounds ridiculous Janie," said
Tommy. "God says let there be
something and then there *just* is? How
does that work? That would be like me

saying, let there be pizza and then '*ta da*', pepperoni pizza appears."

"Only one problem, Tommy," answered Janie. "You're not God!"

"Whatever," mumbled Tommy.

"Look," said Janie, as she pointed to the page. "It says God made the sun and the sky. He made the grass and the fruit trees. He made the fish and the birds. He made all the animals and He made people."

"All by just saying it? I don't know Janie," said Tommy.

"I believe that God can speak and create anything," said Janie. "He's God. Pastor Jack says God is all powerful."

"I'm going to my room," said Tommy. "I have a lot of homework to finish, and it's not going to happen by just *speaking* it. I actually have to do it." He stood up to leave.

"Wait Tommy!" cried Janie. She grabbed Tommy's hand and lowered her head in prayer.

Dear God, I know that You created the world and everything in it with Your voice. Please help my brother believe that too.

"Oh sister," groaned Tommy. "Can I go now?" He turned to leave.

Suddenly, there was a bright flash of light like a lightning bolt, and then a loud booming sound like thunder in the room.

Tommy and Janie fell back and covered their heads with their hands.

They were stunned, unable to move or speak. Then they heard a voice say:

"Fear not, Tommy and Janie. I am an angel sent to you by the one true God!"

2

ANSWERED PRAYER

Standing in the center of Janie's room was a man dressed in a long robe, as white as snow, with a golden belt tied around his waist.

"God heard your prayer Janie, and He has sent me to take you back to the beginning," said the angel.

"The beginning of what?" asked Tommy, who was still trembling with fear.

"The beginning of the earth when God planted a garden of all His creations," replied the angel.

"Oh, you mean the Garden of Eden," said Janie, as she got up to her feet.

"That's right Janie," the angel said.

Tommy got up to his feet too. "So, you know our names, but we don't know yours," said Tommy. "Do angels have names?"

"Yes, we do," said the angel. "My name is Rafael."

"Cool, nice to meet you Rafael," said Tommy.

"So would you both like to go?" asked Rafael.

"Absolutely!" they said at the same time, as twins tend to do.

"Wonderful!" said Rafael. "Let's get right to it."

Suddenly from behind his back, two large white wings appeared and lifted over Rafael's head. "Take my hands and we'll be off," he said.

Tommy and Janie each grabbed one of Rafael's hands. In the twinkling of an eye, they were caught up with a whoosh and were instantly standing in front of a large door. The door was wide open.

Through the door they could see large green mountains way off in the distance, with a bright sun over them. Below the mountains were waterfalls that split off into winding rivers. There were colorful plants, flowers, and trees everywhere.

"Wow, it sure looks like earth, but it's better," said Tommy.

"Yeah, everything is bright and beautiful," said Janie. "It's like the sky and the water are bluer than blue, and the trees and mountains are greener than green."

"The colors of the flowers and plants are amazing!" said Tommy. "And there's not even a cloud in the sky!"

"It is beautiful," said Rafael. "In the beginning everything was pure and clean. There weren't even any clouds yet, because it had never rained."

"How does that work?" asked Tommy. "Everything here would die without rain."

"You'll see," said Rafael, with a smile.

"Can we go in?" asked Tommy and Janie excitedly.

"Of course, go and explore on your own!" said Rafael. "There's nothing in there that can hurt you. Have fun!"

"Okay, we'll see you later!" said Tommy. And they ran off through the great door.

3

EXPLORING THE GARDEN

"Over here Janie!" called Tommy. "I see a waterfall!"

Just past the door was a small waterfall attached to a winding river. Tommy and Janie walked up to it and let the water run over their hands. Then they both made cups with their hands and had a drink.

"Mmm," said Tommy. "Now that's *good* water."

"That *is good* water," said Janie.

"Way better than what comes out of our sink at home," said Tommy.

Below the waterfall in the river were fish of all different sizes and shapes.

"Tommy, look at the fish in the river!" said Janie. "There's so many of them."

"Wow," said Tommy. "They're so colorful! And the water is so clear you can see all the way to the bottom. Amazing!"

"Dad would love this," said Janie. "It would be very easy for him to catch fish here."

Tommy and Janie put their hands in the river. To their surprise many of the fish swam towards them. Then the fish

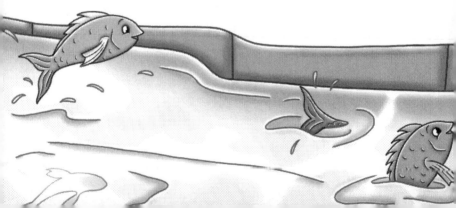

started playing with their hands, swimming in circles and even jumping out of the water near them.

"What are they doing?" asked Tommy.

"I don't know," said Janie. "But they sure seem to like us."

Just then a bright blue fish jumped out of the water and into Tommy's hands. Another green fish jumped into Janie's hands. They wiggled and jiggled playfully as Tommy and Janie laughed.

"Well, it looks like the fish catch themselves here in the Garden of Eden," said Tommy. "No need for fishing poles at all."

Then Tommy spotted a small white lamb sipping water from the river.

"Look across the river Janie," said Tommy. "It's a baby lamb."

"Aww, I wonder where its mother is," said Janie.

As the lamb kept drinking, a giant lion suddenly came out of the trees behind it. Tommy and Janie stood frozen and watched in horror as the lion crept up on the tiny lamb.

"I don't know, but I'm pretty sure that's not its mommy," gulped Tommy. "It's about to get ugly, real ugly."

They were sure the lion was about to devour the baby lamb for a meal. The lion kept coming towards the lamb. But to their complete surprise, it walked up alongside the lamb and began to drink from the river too.

When the lion had finished drinking, it turned around and went into some tall grass near the river and laid down in the sun. Then the lamb turned towards the lion, walked over, and curled up next to it. They both closed their eyes for a nap.

"Wow, that's a relief!" said Janie.

"Actually, that's impossible!" said Tommy. "It doesn't make any sense. Lions eat lambs, plain and simple. And it should eat us too if the river wasn't between us."

"I guess Rafael is right. Maybe there is nothing in here that can hurt us," said Janie.

4

WATER EVERYWHERE

Tommy and Janie walked up the riverbed to see what else they could find.

They were amazed. To their left and right were trees of every color imaginable. There were orange trees, lemon trees, plum trees, cherry trees, peach trees, lime trees and so many more. In between the trees were beautiful flowers just as colorful.

"This place is absolutely incredible!" said Janie.

"Yeah, there's so much food here. Mom would never have to go to the grocery store again!" said Tommy. "Let's try some peaches!"

Tommy ran to a peach tree and climbed up to where the fruit was. He dropped one down to Janie and then climbed down with his. They both took a bite.

"Mmm, that's the peachiest peach I've ever tasted," said Janie.

"Wow, that *is good*!" said Tommy.

They each gobbled down their peaches.

"Let's go see what else we can find," said Janie. They walked off in search of more fruit to eat.

As they were walking, water suddenly began to burst up from the ground.

"Yikes!" yelled Tommy. "Who turned on the sprinklers?"

Tommy and Janie began to run to get away from the water, but the water was everywhere all at once. Instead of running, they began dancing and playing. They got soaked!

And then just as suddenly as the water began, it stopped.

"Whoa, the water just came straight up from the ground!" laughed Janie.

"Only I can't find any sprinklers," said Tommy. "That is so weird."

Just then an older man walked up to them. He had a long white beard. He wore a plain brown robe with a rope tied around his waist.

"Looks like you two got caught in the water," said the man with a smile.

"Yeah," said Tommy. "The water just shot up everywhere from the ground."

"Sorry about that," said the man. "But the garden does need to be watered."

"That's okay," said Janie. "It was actually fun."

"You like it here?" asked the man.

"Oh yes," said Janie. "Very much!"

"I can't wait to see more," said Tommy.

"Wonderful, I'm glad you're both enjoying yourselves. There are some towels over there under that lemon tree," said the man, as he pointed behind them. "You're welcome to dry off a bit."

Tommy and Janie turned to look for the lemon tree. Seeing the towels, they turned back to thank the man, but he was gone.

"Where did he go so fast?" asked Tommy. "And who was he?"

"I don't know, maybe he's the gardener," said Janie. "He sure had kind eyes."

Tommy and Janie went over to the lemon tree and dried off with the towels. Then they went off in search of more fruit to eat.

5

CRAZY BIRDS

"Oh, look Tommy!" said Janie. "I think those are pomegranates on that tree. My friend had one at school."

"Pome-what?" answered Tommy.

"Pomegranates," repeated Janie. "Give me a boost up and I'll get a couple for us."

Tommy made a step for her with his hands and pulled her up high enough to reach two fruits.

"How do I open it, Janie?" asked Tommy.

"Just pull it apart, kind of like an orange," replied Janie.

Tommy dug his nails into the outer skin and ripped his pomegranate open. Inside were dark red seeds.

"You eat the seeds Tommy," said Janie. "Try one!"

Tommy popped one in his mouth.

"Oh, they taste kind of like cherries," said Tommy.

As Tommy and Janie were eating their fruit seeds, a few medium sized brightly colored birds came flying over to them. One landed smack on top of Tommy's head.

"Whoa!" yelled Tommy. "What is this crazy bird doing?" He held very still because he was afraid the bird was going to claw his head off.

"It's okay Tommy," said Janie. "I think it just wants some of your pomegranate seeds." She held up a handful of seeds near the bird. The bird ate right out of her hand.

"Whew!" said Tommy. "It only wants the fruit."

Just then another bird swooped down and landed on Janie's arm so it could eat out of her hand too. Then many more of the same kind of bird came and landed all over and around Tommy and Janie.

They fed them all the best they could.

"I don't know what kind of birds these are," said Janie.

"Yeah, they're colorful, but they're too small to be parrots and too big to be parakeets," said Tommy.

After all the seeds had been eaten, the birds did not fly away. They stayed nearby in the trees and on the ground. Some even stayed on their arms and Tommy and Janie began to stroke their feathers.

"Why aren't these birds afraid of us Janie?" asked Tommy. "Birds don't come anywhere near us at home."

"I have no idea Tommy," answered Janie.

"This is one strange place," said Tommy. "Birds let us feed and pet them. Fish jump right out of the water and into our hands. And lions and lambs snuggle up together for a nap. It doesn't make any sense."

"Rafael was definitely right," said Janie. "There is nothing in here that can hurt us."

"This is so much fun," said Tommy. "Let's keep exploring upstream!"

6

ADAM AND EVE

Tommy and Janie made their way through plants and brightly colored flowers that were almost as tall as them. They began to hear talking and went towards the voices.

When they got close, they were able to see two men through the plants. One was the man in the brown robe who gave them the towels. On his shoulder was a bird like the ones they had just fed. He was talking to a much younger man.

Tommy and Janie stayed well hidden in the tall plants and listened.

"Adam, I came across a kind of bird today that you haven't named yet," said the man. He handed it over. "What do you think it should be called?" he asked.

"Well, it's bigger than a parakeet and smaller than a parrot," said Adam.

"That's exactly what I said," whispered Tommy to his sister.

"I think I'd like to call it a lorikeet," said Adam.

"Then a lorikeet it shall be," said the man.

"Tommy, that's Adam," whispered Janie. "You know Adam, like Adam and Eve, the first humans."

"Well, that other guy is definitely not Eve," whispered Tommy. "Who is he?"

"I don't know," whispered Janie. "I still think he's the gardener."

"I ran across these lorikeets on my way here. Apparently, they like pomegranate seeds," said the man with a smile.

"I'll remember that," said Adam. "See you later this evening."

With that Adam turned and headed up the river with the lorikeet on his shoulder. The man in the brown robe walked the other way.

"How does he know that lorikeets like pomegranate seeds unless he was watching us?" asked Tommy.

"I have no idea," answered Janie. "Maybe he just wants to keep an eye on us."

"Yeah maybe," said Tommy. "Let's follow Adam and see where he goes."

"Good idea," said Janie. "Maybe we'll get to see Eve."

They continued up the river in the direction that Adam had gone. As they walked, they came to a large open area with tall grass and flowers. In the very middle of the clearing were two giant trees. They were much larger than any of the other trees they had seen in the garden.

Adam was making his way to one of the trees, which had huge red apples on it. Under that tree was a woman resting in the shade of its branches.

Tommy and Janie stopped short of the trees and stayed hidden.

"Tommy, that must be Eve!" said Janie.

7

TROUBLE AT THE TREE

"Hi Eve, how's it going honey?" asked Adam. He bent down and kissed the top of her head.

"Going well, what have you been up to sweetie?" asked Eve. She looked up at him and smiled. "And what is that on your shoulder?"

"It's a lorikeet!" said Adam proudly. "I got to name it today."

"Aww, it's really cute and colorful," said Eve.

"They are a really sweet couple," said Janie. "You can tell they're in love."

Tommy rolled his eyes. "They're a bit much for me," said Tommy. "Nobody's that nice to each other."

Just then, as Adam stood near Eve, a snake slithered up. Eve was not afraid of it though, and she even started talking to it. Even more weird is that the snake started talking too.

"Um, Janie," said Tommy. "Is Eve really talking to that snake, and is that snake actually talking back?"

"Oh no," said Janie. "I know this story from the Bible. This is *not good*."

They began to listen more closely to their conversation.

The snake said, "Did God really say you can't eat from every tree in the Garden?"

Eve answered, "We may eat the fruit from all the trees except *this* one. If we eat from it, God says we will die."

The snake said, "You won't die. God knows your eyes will be open and you will be like God, knowing good and evil."

Eve stood up and looked at the fruit of the tree. Then she pulled a great red apple off and stared at it in her hands.

"Oh no," said Janie. "She's not supposed to eat that fruit."

Finally, Eve *did* take a bite of the fruit. Then she handed it to Adam, and he ate too. They both just stood there looking at each other. The snake slithered away.

"What just happened Janie?" asked Tommy. "I'm so confused."

"Adam and Eve ate the fruit that God told them not to," said Janie.

Suddenly, Adam's face got really red. "Why did you give me that fruit to eat woman?" he screamed.

"The snake tricked me!" Eve yelled back. "Why didn't you stop me?"

"God's going to be really mad at us EVE!" screamed Adam. "He said we'll die!"

"Isn't God going to be here soon?" cried Eve.

"We'd better hide!" yelled Adam.

Adam and Eve ran off behind the large trees.

Tommy and Janie sat motionless in the tall grass. Suddenly, the man in the brown robe walked up behind them.

"The Garden is no longer safe for you," he said. "You need to go."

"Why isn't it safe here anymore?" asked Tommy.

"The Garden has been broken by what you have just seen done today. It will affect everything," said the man. "Make your way back down the river to the door." The man turned and walked on his way.

"I don't get it Janie," said Tommy. "All they did was eat an apple. I don't want to leave. Except for Adam and Eve yelling at each other, this place is awesome."

"I think we better start heading back Tommy," said Janie.

8

A BROKEN WORLD

Tommy and Janie began to make their way back downstream to where the fruit trees were.

"Let's have one more piece of fruit before we go," said Tommy.

"Okay," said Janie. "How about a pear?"

"Sounds good," said Tommy. "I'll climb up."

Tommy started up the tree, but when he got to the lowest branches he cried out in pain.

"There's thorns all over up here! I can't get to the fruit," he said.

"Come down Tommy," said Janie. "You're gonna get hurt."

"No, I got this," said Tommy, as he reached for a different pear. "Oww!" screeched Tommy. "That one really got me! My hand is bleeding."

"Tommy, forget it!" yelled Janie. "It's not worth it."

Tommy came back down the pear tree without any fruit.

"Let's go," sighed Tommy.

"Is your hand alright?" asked Janie.

"Yeah," said Tommy. "I'll just rinse it off in the river. It'll be fine."

Tommy went and washed the blood off his hand.

"Look down in the water Janie," said Tommy. "You can't see the bottom anymore."

"Eww, it's kinda dirty," said Janie.

"I wonder why?" said Tommy.

"No idea," said Janie.

"Let's go see the lorikeets on our way out," said Tommy.

They walked on down the riverbed.

"Oh, look Tommy," said Janie. "There they are! The lorikeets are still at the pomegranate tree."

"What on earth are they doing?" asked Tommy.

Tommy and Janie watched as the lorikeets swarmed around the pomegranate tree. They were plucking off all the fruit. The fruit fell to the ground and smashed open.

Then the lorikeets began fighting each other over the seeds. They would swoop down and smash each other. They pecked each other violently.

"They're acting nuts," said Janie. "I'm not going near them."

"Are those really the same birds that ate out of our hands and let us pet them?" asked Tommy.

"They are," sighed Janie. "I really wanted to feed them some more seeds."

"Looks like they've had all the pomegranate seeds they can handle," said Tommy.

"What a mess," said Janie. "Let's go."

"Yeah," said Tommy. "This place isn't as much fun as it used to be."

9

REAL UGLY

Tommy and Janie arrived back at the waterfall. Janie cupped her hands for some more water. She took a sip and then spit it out.

"Tommy, this water tastes bad," said Janie. "It's nasty."

Tommy also tried some water and then spit it back out. "Yeah, you're right. It's not good. It tastes like dirt."

Janie looked down into the cloudy water. "Where did all the fish go?" she asked.

lay. Drool fell from its mouth. It stood directly over the baby lamb.

"Janie, you need to turn around and face the other way right now," Tommy said calmly.

"But Tommy," whimpered Janie. "The lamb..."

"Trust me on this one Janie," said Tommy. "You don't want to see this."

"Ok," sighed Janie.

Janie turned around and put her thumbs in her ears. She was sobbing uncontrollably.

Tommy kept watching as the lion picked up the baby lamb with its large sharp fangs of its mouth and shook it fiercely. Blood sprayed out from the lamb. Then the lion turned towards the trees and carried the bloody lamb away.

"It's over Janie," said Tommy. "They're gone now." He put his hand on her shoulder to comfort her.

"What happened?" asked Janie. "Is the baby lamb alive? Did it get away?"

Tommy shook his head no. "It got ugly Janie, real ugly," he said. "We need to get out of here now. This place is scary!"

10

THE SNAKE AT THE

DOOR

Tommy and Janie ran without stopping all the way to the door of the Garden.

They were about to go through, but there was a snake blocking their way, and they stopped. It was the same snake that had talked to Eve.

"Hello there," it snarled.

"Uh, hello," said Tommy, as they both took a step back.

"Leaving so soon?" asked the snake.

"The gardener told us to leave," said Janie. "He said it's not safe here anymore."

"The gardener, huh?" said the snake. "That's nonsense. You'll be safe with me."

The snake slithered towards them. Tommy and Janie didn't know what to do. They had to get to the door.

"Safe with you?" said Janie. "You tricked Adam and Eve into disobeying God's rules. You've ruined everything!"

"I didn't eat the apple, *they* did," said the snake. "And nothing is ruined. In fact, things are finally going right."

"Nothing is right here anymore," said Tommy. "The Garden was incredible, and now it's just like home.

"That's right," said the snake. "It is just like home. So why don't you stay with me here?"

The snake crept closer. Tommy and Janie couldn't get to the door.

"No, we're leaving!" said Janie. "Pastor Jack says you're a liar!"

"A liar?" laughed the snake. "I think you have me confused with someone else."

"No, you're the devil," said Janie. "You may have tricked Eve, but I know who you are. I've heard about you."

"We're leaving," said Tommy.

"Actually, you're not going anywhere," said the snake.

At that, the snake moved right up to them, raised its head, and began to hiss.

Tommy and Janie turned to run away, but behind them a lion appeared from behind a tree.

"You remember my friend here from the river," said the snake. "The baby lamb was just a snack. He's still hungry."

Tommy and Janie stood paralyzed with fear...

"BEGONE SERPENT!"

yelled the gardener, seemingly coming out of nowhere.

Immediately the lion turned and ran off. The snake dropped back to the ground and slithered away into the grass.

"Wow," said Tommy to the gardener. "All you did was tell that snake to leave and it left."

"Thank you so much," said Janie.

"You're welcome, Tommy and Janie," said the man. "You better get going, Rafael is waiting to take you both home. Oh, and Tommy, I'm sending a surprise for you when you get there."

Tommy and Janie looked at each other in confusion. When they looked back to the gardener, he was already gone.

11

HOME AGAIN

Rafael stepped into the doorway to greet them. Tommy and Janie were so happy to see him they ran up and hugged his robe.

"So how was your adventure?" asked Rafael.

"It was wonderful," said Tommy. "We played with fish and birds. We got rescued from a snake and a lion."

"It was awful," said Janie. "The birds went crazy, and the fish and the lamb died."

"Well, which was it, good or bad?" asked Rafael.

"Both," they said together.

"You should have seen it, Rafael." said Tommy.

"The snake wanted to kill us. The gardener saved our lives!"

"Wow," smiled Rafael. "That is incredible."

"But Rafael, how did that gardener know our names?" asked Janie.

"Well,"answered Rafael. "You see...

"And how did he know you were waiting for us?" interrupted Tommy.

"Kids," said Rafael. "That wasn't just *any* gardener."

"That's for sure," said Tommy. "He saved us from a snake and a lion just by yelling at them!"

"Tommy and Janie, that gardener was God," said Rafael.

"What, that's amazing!" said Janie. "I had no idea."

"You see, God walked and talked with Adam and Eve in the Garden," said Rafael.

"Wow," said Tommy. "He talked to us too."

"Yes, He did," said Rafael. "But we need to get going now. Take my hands."

Tommy and Janie each held one of Rafael's hands. In the twinkling of an eye, they were caught up with a whoosh and were instantly back in Janie's room.

"It's time for me to go," said Rafael.

"Thank you so much for taking us!" Janie said.

"My pleasure," said Rafael. And he was gone.

"Well Tommy," said Janie. What do you think about our adventure?"

"It was awesome!" said Tommy. "I saw the beginning of the world all with my own eyes. But I still don't believe God *spoke* everything into existence."

Just then there was a voice in the room, and it said,

"Let there be pizza!"

Immediately on the bed in front of them, a freshly baked pepperoni pizza appeared out of thin air.

The voice spoke again,

"Tada!"

"I know that voice," said Tommy. "It's the gardener's voice. It's God's voice!"

"I wouldn't believe this if I wasn't seeing it with my own eyes and hearing it with my own ears," said Tommy. "Now I do believe that God really did create the world with His voice!"

Janie looked up and silently thanked God for answering her prayer.

"Wow, God was in the Garden with us," said Janie. "He spoke to us, gave us towels, watched over us, warned us, and protected us. God is so good Tommy," said Janie.

"I bet He makes good pizza too!" laughed Tommy.

"Let's eat!"they said.

From the Author's Desk

Hi Kids,

I wanted to let you know that although this story is fictional, His Story (meaning God's Story) is true. You see God really did create a perfect world for us. Adam and Eve were real people who disobeyed God. In fact, we all break His rules, and we live in a broken world because of it.

But God loves us all so much that He isn't willing to leave us like this. He has a good plan to rescue you and me. As you read the next few adventures with Tommy and Janie, you'll see how His saving plan unfolds. Trust me, it's good news!

Jen Decker

Adventures in His Story
Book 2

FROM BAD TO WORSE

What's the big deal? Adam and Eve just ate an apple...
Find out for yourselves, as Rafael the angel swoops in again and takes Tommy and Janie back in time on another adventure.

COMING SOON!